# Karen's Cartwheel

# Look for these
## and other books about Karen
## in the
## Baby-sitters Little Sister series:

# 1  Karen's Witch

# 2  Karen's Roller Skates

# 3  Karen's Worst Day

# 4  Karen's Kittycat Club

# 5  Karen's School Picture

# 6  Karen's Little Sister

# 7  Karen's Birthday

# 8  Karen's Haircut

# 9  Karen's Sleepover

#10  Karen's Grandmothers

#11  Karen's Prize

#12  Karen's Ghost

#13  Karen's Surprise

#14  Karen's New Year

#15  Karen's in Love

#16  Karen's Goldfish

#17  Karen's Brothers

#18  Karen's Home Run

#19  Karen's Good-bye

#20  Karen's Carnival

#21  Karen's New Teacher

#22  Karen's Little Witch

#23  Karen's Doll

#24  Karen's School Trip

#25  Karen's Pen Pal

#26  Karen's Ducklings

#27  Karen's Big Joke

#28  Karen's Tea Party

#29  Karen's Cartwheel

#30  Karen's Kittens

Super Specials:

# 1  Karen's Wish

# 2  Karen's Plane Trip

# 3  Karen's Mystery

## Little Sister

# Karen's Cartwheel
## Ann M. Martin

Illustrations by Susan Tang

A
**LITTLE APPLE**
PAPERBACK

SCHOLASTIC INC.
New York Toronto London Auckland Sydney

ISBN 0-590-44825-0

12 11 10 9 8 7 6 5 4 3 2 1          2 3 4 5 6 7/9

Printed in the U.S.A.                    40

First Scholastic printing, June 1992

*For Grace Polywoda*

# Karen's Cartwheel

# The Best

"And . . . over you go!" said Miss Donovan.

"Oof," I huffed.

Miss Donovan is my gymnastics teacher. She was helping me turn a cartwheel. I am pretty good at gymnastics. I am the only one in my class who can almost do a back flip on the mat. But I cannot turn a cartwheel. Everyone else can. Even Natalie Springer, who is mostly a klutz.

When Miss Donovan helped *me* go over,

1

I bent my waist. My legs flopped. And I had tried really hard. I had done my best. But my best was terrible when I was turning cartwheels. (To make myself feel better, I tried a back flip.)

I am Karen Brewer. I am seven years old. I adore gymnastics. I adore Miss Donovan, too. And I like the kids in my class. They are Sophie, Gemma, Gregg, Polly, Jannie, and Natalie. Guess what. Jannie and Natalie are also in my class at regular school. We go to Stoneybrook Academy. We are in second grade. Our teacher is Ms. Colman, and she is soooo nice.

"Boys and girls!" called Miss Donovan. (Really, only one boy is in my gymnastics class. Gregg. But I guess Miss Donovan would have felt funny saying "Boy and girls" or "Girls and boy.") "We have ten minutes left before class ends. Please use the time to practice. Remember that the invitational team will be chosen soon."

I remembered. How could I forget? More than anything else in the world I wanted to be on the invitational gymnastics team. The team is special. It is for really good gymnasts. And only a few kids from each class would be chosen for the team. It was called an invitational team because the teachers *invited* you to be on it — if you were good enough. You could not try out for the team. You just had to be asked.

For several weeks the teachers at gymnastics school had been watching the kids in every class. They were *observing*, Miss Donovan said. Soon they would announce the names of the kids they would invite to join the team. I just *had* to be one of those kids! The special team got to do cool things. They got to go to meets in other towns, and they rode to the meets on a bus. Sometimes they put on gymnastics shows. I just love being in shows. I thought I would probably be invited to join the special team. I am usually the best at anything I try. I knew I was not Miss Donovan's best gymnast, though. Plus, I have that cartwheel problem.

Well, the way to get better is to practice. So I did.

Gemma and I practiced hard during those last ten minutes. We were still practicing when I looked up and saw . . .

"Seth!" I cried.

"Hi, honey." Seth waved to me. "I'll wait here until you are ready." He sat on a bench in the hall with some parents and baby-sitters.

"Okay!" I said.

Gemma and I were using the balance beam. Gemma was walking across it backward. I was spotting her. (That means I was staying with her in case she fell or needed help.)

When Gemma reached the end, I took my last turn on the beam. Then I ran to Seth. Seth is my stepfather. He had come to drive me home. I mean, to one of my homes. I have two houses. And I call myself Karen Two-Two. This is why.

# The Best Two-Two

Once, a long time ago, when I was in preschool, I was still a one-one, like most of my friends. I had one family — Mommy, Daddy, me, and my little brother, Andrew — and we lived in one house. Then something happened. Mommy and Daddy got a divorce. They decided they did not want to live together because they did not love each other anymore. So Mommy moved out of the big house where we had been living. (It is the house Daddy grew up in.) She moved to a little house not far away. It is even in the same town, which is Stoneybrook, in the state of Connecticut. Then she got married again. She married Seth. That is how he became my stepfather. Daddy got married again, too. He married Elizabeth, my stepmother.

Remember I said that Mommy and Daddy did not love each other anymore? That was why they got divorced. But Mommy and Daddy still loved Andrew and me very much. And *that* is how we got to be two-twos. Mommy and Daddy both wanted us to live with them. So now Andrew and I live with Mommy at the little house most of the time. And we live with Daddy at the big house every other weekend and on some vacations and holidays.

I am very good at being a two-two.

Here is who is in my little-house family: Mommy, Seth, Andrew, me, Rocky and Midgie (Seth's cat and dog), and Emily Junior. Emily is my very own rat.

Here is who is in my big-house family: Daddy, Elizabeth, Kristy, Charlie, Sam,

David Michael, Emily Michelle, Nannie, Shannon, Boo-Boo, Goldfishie, and Crystal Light the Second. Whew! Kristy, Charlie, Sam, and David Michael are Elizabeth's four kids, so they are my stepsister and stepbrothers. Charlie and Sam go to high school. David Michael is seven, like me (but he is a few months older). And Kristy is thirteen and one of my favorite, favorite people. She baby-sits. She is lots of fun. Emily Michelle is my adopted sister. (I named my rat after her.) Daddy and Elizabeth adopted her from a faraway country called Vietnam. Emily is two and a half. She is very cute, but she does not talk much. Nannie is Elizabeth's mother. (That makes her my stepgrandmother.) She helps take care of Emily Michelle. Let me see. Oh, yes. The pets. Shannon is David Michael's puppy. Boo-Boo is Daddy's cross old cat. And Goldfishie and Crystal Light the Second are the fish that belong to Andrew and me.

As a two-two I have two families, two

houses, two mommies, two daddies, two cats, and two dogs. I also have two best friends. Hannie Papadakis lives near Daddy. Nancy Dawes lives next door to Mommy. (My best friends are also in Ms. Colman's second-grade class with me.) Plus, I have two bicycles, one at each house. And I have clothes and toys and books at each house. I hardly have to pack anything when I go from one house to the other.

Of course, I do not have two of *everything*. I only have one pair of roller skates. And I only have one rat. When I am at Daddy's, I miss Emily Junior and my little-house family. When I am at Mommy's, I miss my big-house family. Here is one thing I do not miss. I do not miss Morbidda Destiny. She is the witch who lives next door to Daddy. She is very scary. Luckily, I do not have to see her too often.

# Karen Onstage

"*We're off to see the mall! The best mall of all!*" I sang.

It was a Saturday, a big-house Saturday. Daddy and Elizabeth had planned a special treat. A new toy store had opened in Washington Mall. They were taking Emily Michelle, David Michael, Andrew, Nancy, Hannie, and me to see it.

Washington Mall is far away. We had to drive for one half of an *hour* to get there. But I entertained everybody. I made up new songs like the one about going to see the mall. Also, I told a couple of jokes.

Finally Daddy turned off the highway. He drove into the parking lot at the mall. Soon we were going inside. Hannie and Nancy and I ran ahead. We call ourselves the Three Musketeers. That is because we are best friends and we are usually together.

"I love the mall!" exclaimed Hannie.

"Breathe deeply," I said. "I can smell popcorn and new shoes and pizza and ice cream and perfume and the haircutting place."

Hannie and Nancy breathed in. "Scrumptious," said Nancy.

"Girls, stay with us!" called Daddy.

My friends and I waited until the others had caught up.

"Are we going right to the toy store?" I asked. "Or could we get something to eat first? I am an intsy bit hungry."

"Me, too," said Andrew, David Michael, Emily, Hannie, and Nancy.

10

"You may each have one snack while we are at the mall," said Elizabeth.

Guess what. Each of us wanted a different snack. David Michael wanted a slice of pizza, Andrew wanted an ice-cream cone, Nancy wanted an Orange Julius, Hannie wanted popcorn, Emily wanted M&M's, and I was hoping to find a place that sold cotton candy.

"This would be easier," said Daddy, "if you all wanted to eat the same thing."

But we didn't. Luckily we found a stand that sold everything we wanted. Except cotton candy. I settled for an Orange Julius, like Nancy.

Here is a great thing about malls. You can walk around and eat your food at the same time. You do not have to sit in a chair until you are finished.

First we walked to the pet store. We stood outside and watched the puppies in the window. They frisked around and touched their wet noses to everything. One of them fell asleep on his back.

"Daddy? Can we get a puppy?" I asked.

"Absolutely not," he said.

And Elizabeth added, "What would Shannon think?"

Next we went to the magic shop. In the window stood a toy magician. Over and over, he pulled a stuffed rabbit out of a top hat.

"Daddy?" I said.

"No, we cannot buy any magic tricks."

Darn. How did he know I was going to ask for one?

We were on our way to the toy store when I saw a crowd of people.

"Hey! What's going on?" I cried. We hurried over to the people. "I see gymnastics stuff!" I said. "I see a balance beam and a horse and a lot of mats. Oh, and some parallel bars."

Eight kids were putting on a gymnastics show. They were just a little older than me. They must be on a special team, I thought. I bet they are on an invitational team. This must be one of the things they get to do.

I imagined myself on the balance beam, performing in front of the people at the mall. That would be so, so cool. (I simply adore having an audience.) Maybe, I thought, when I am on the invitational team, I will get to perform at malls.

But first, I remembered, I would have to learn to turn a cartwheel.

# Carolina, Eugenia, and Petrolia

We watched the gymnastics team until we had finished our snacks. The kids were extra good. They could do roundoffs. They could flip off the beam and land on their feet (not on their bottoms). And they could sail over the horse, and twirl around those bars.

When our snacks had disappeared, Daddy said, "Time to find the toy store."

The new store was called Toy Palace, and it was easy to find. Bunches of balloons were tied in front of it. A clown was walking around. He was juggling apples. A gigundo lion (not a real one) was walking around, too. He smiled at Andrew. He patted Emily on the head. (Emily cried.)

"I have an idea," I said to Nancy and Hannie. "When we get inside, let's walk down every aisle, in order, so we do not miss one single toy."

"Okay," agreed my friends.

We started at one side of the store. Against the wall were bicycles and tricycles and riding toys. We walked slowly to the end of the aisle. Then we turned down the next one. It was the game aisle. We looked and looked and looked. And we took our time. Daddy and Elizabeth had said we could walk around by ourselves if we promised not to leave the store.

Nancy and Hannie and I looked at the Lego aisle. We looked at the arts and crafts aisle. We looked at the truck and car aisle and the baby toy aisle and the video game aisle. At last we came to . . .

"Dolls!" cried Nancy.

We were surrounded by dolls. They were stacked up from the beginning of the aisle to the end. Dolls, dolls, dolls.

"This one walks her very own puppy!" exclaimed Hannie.

"This one can crawl," said Nancy.

"This one comes with dress-ups," I said.

We saw bride dolls and princess dolls and doctor dolls and baby dolls. We even saw an astronaut doll. Then I saw a very wonderful doll. She was not a princess or anything. She was just a girl wearing blue jeans. She looked a lot like me.

"You guys!" I said to Hannie and Nancy.

"Wow!" said Nancy softly. "Cool." And Hannie added, "She looks like you. And this one with the brown hair looks kind of like Nancy and me. And here's one with red hair, and here's one with black hair."

I checked the doll's price tag. "She does not cost *too* much," I said. "Not even fourteen dollars. She is just thirteen ninety-five."

"If this one were mine," said Nancy, "I would name her Carolina."

"I would name her Eugenia," said Hannie.

"*I* would name her Petrolia."

"You know," said Nancy, "if each of us bought one of those dolls, we could have triplets. We could call them the Doll Sisters."

My eyes grew wide. What a gigundoly terrific idea! "I am going to ask Daddy for money right now!" I cried.

Guess what. Daddy would not buy those dolls for my friends and me. He said they cost a little too much. But he said that if we earned enough money to buy the Doll Sisters, he would drive Hannie and Nancy and me back to the mall so we could pick them out.

Hmm.

"I think we can do that," said Hannie. We were on our way home. Each of us was holding a free balloon from the clown. Our car looked like a birthday party.

"Yeah," agreed Nancy. "We could do that."

"And then we could have sleepovers with the Doll Sisters," I said.

"We could make clothes for them. Matching clothes," said Hannie.

"We could take them on bike rides," I added. "Awesome. And all we have to do is earn a little over forty dollars."

# Pennies and Nickels

As soon as Elizabeth pulled into the driveway at the big house, Nancy and Hannie and I flew out of the car.

"I have an idea!" I whispered loudly.

"What is it?" asked Hannie.

"Shh! I will tell you in a minute. Come to my room."

When we were safely in my room, I closed the door.

"I know where we can get some money," I said.

21

"Where?" asked Nancy and Hannie.

"We can look for it in our houses. We can look under the couch cushions and under chairs and in cars," I said. "Any money like that is yours. Finders keepers. Because you don't know who it really belongs to."

"We can go on a treasure hunt!" exclaimed Nancy.

So we did. We started at Daddy's house. We started in the den. "People sit in here more than anywhere else in the house," I told my friends.

First we crawled around on the floor. We looked under the furniture. And do you know what? Right away I found a nickel! Then we felt around the cushions in the couch and the chairs.

"Gross," said Nancy. "All I feel are crumbs. And here's something sticky." She pulled it out. "Oh, yuck. I think it's a piece of gum."

"Chewed?" asked Hannie.

"Nope. Dust covered."

But then Hannie found a penny and Nancy found a *quarter*.

"Cool!" I cried. "Thirty-one cents!"

By the time we had looked all over the house, we had found fifty-four cents. (And a pen Kristy had lost, and two of Boo-Boo's toys.)

"Let's go to my house now," said Hannie.

"Okay. But first we will empty my piggy bank," I said.

Inside it, we found eighty-five cents. Now we had one dollar and thirty-nine cents. We put our money in one of my socks and carried the sock to Hannie's. Then we searched all over Hannie's house. When we had finished we had found eight pennies, three dimes, a nickel, and another quarter.

"And a nail," said Hannie.

"And a dried-up macaroni," said Nancy.

"Okay, let's open my bank!" exclaimed Hannie.

Hannie's bank is gigundoly cool. It looks like a big red mouth. When you drop some money through the lips, the bank says, "Mmm. That was yummy!" and, "Please feed me again!" When we emptied it, the bank said, "Don't forget to feed me soon!"

Hannie had put forty-eight cents in her lip bank. We added up our money. A dollar thirty-nine plus sixty-eight cents (finders keepers), plus forty-eight cents (lip bank) equals two dollars and fifty-five cents.

"Not bad," I said. "Nancy, when you go home, look around your house and in your bank, okay?"

"Okay," she replied.

Nancy telephoned me after dinner. "I found one dollar and twenty cents," she said proudly. "And I added everything up. We have *three seventy-five*."

"Wow! Now we just have to earn . . . Let me see." I figured it out on paper. "Well, we still have to earn thirty-eight dollars and ten cents."

"Thirty-eight dollars!" cried Nancy.

"And ten cents," I added.

"Boo."

So then we asked for advances on our allowances, but our parents said no.

Double boo.

6

# Waiting

"Guess what, girls and . . . um, girls and Gregg," said Miss Donovan.

"What?" we replied. I stopped halfway across the balance beam. My gymnastics teacher stood in the middle of our room.

"You can relax a little," she said with a smile. (I hopped off the beam.) "The judges have finished watching our classes. Now they are deciding who to ask to join the invitational team. When you come to our next class, I will announce the names. I want you to know that I think you all worked hard."

I did not know whether to feel happy or sad. I felt partly happy because I could not wait to hear Miss Donovan call my name to tell me I had been asked to join the special team. Soon I would be performing in malls. But I felt partly sad because I was still working on my cartwheels. I had wanted the judges to see my *best* cartwheels, and I knew they had not. Oh, well. Too late now.

Miss Donovan was still talking to our class. I tried to pay attention to her, but I could not. I was busy daydreaming. I could see pictures in my head. I saw Miss Donovan saying, "I am happy to ask Karen Brewer to join the invitational team." Then I saw myself standing up. Tears were in my eyes. "Oh, how can I ever thank you?" I said. (I put my hand over my heart.) "This means more to me than anything in the world." Next I saw myself at Mommy's house. When I told her the good news, she wept. She hugged me to her. Then I phoned Daddy. He cried, too. "When you are turning cartwheels at the mall," he said, "I will bring the entire family to see you. I will tell people, 'That's my daughter.' "

"Karen? Karen?"

I shook my head. Natalie Springer was tugging at my elbow.

"Yeah?"

"We are supposed to be working on our floor routines," said Natalie. "Miss Donovan told me to be your partner. Come on."

Natalie and I practiced and practiced. It is a good thing Miss Donovan puts mats on the floor. Natalie falls a lot.

But not me. I did not start falling until Miss Donovan added a cartwheel to the routine. Then, flip-flop. I was on my bottom more than I was on my hands or my feet.

Those darn old cartwheels. I did not give up, though. I worked and worked and worked. Miss Donovan said she was proud of me.

# Odd Jobs

"Karen!" Mommy called. "Telephone!"

"Coming!" I called back. I was in my room at the little house. Gymnastics class was over. I was daydreaming about the invitational team again. It was the part of the dream where Daddy says he will bring the entire family to watch me perform at the mall. I changed the dream just a little. Now when Daddy says he will bring the family, he breaks down and sobs. He is sobbing because he is so very, very happy. He is so proud of his daughter Karen the invitational gymnast.

I ran into Mommy and Seth's room. I picked up the phone. "Hello?"

"Hi, it's me." Hannie was calling. "Guess what. I was talking to Nancy. We had a great idea. We know how to earn money to buy the Doll Sisters."

"How?" I asked. "How?"

"We will start a business. We will do chores and odd jobs for people. We will walk their dogs. We will clean their houses. We will weed their gardens. We will do anything they need done."

"That is excellent!" I cried. "We will tell our families about our business."

"And our neighbors," said Hannie. "They will probably have jobs for us."

"We can call everyone we know!" I said. "Also, we can make posters. We can put them up near our houses."

"Cool," said Hannie. "Let's get to work."

We got to work on Saturday. Hannie and Nancy came to the big house. (Andrew and

I were there for the weekend.) We sat on the floor in my room. We made posters. This is what they said:

GIRLS CAN DO ANYTHING!
CALL THE ODD-JOB SERVICE!
KAREN, NANCY, AND HANNIE!
REMEMBER . . .
GIRLS CAN DO ANYTHING!! (REALLY)

We listed our phone numbers on the bottom of each poster.

"How many posters should we make?" asked Nancy.

"About forty," I answered.

We made three. We decided to put up two near Daddy's house. Nancy said she would take hers home with her. She would put it up near the little house.

We waited for the phone to start ringing.

By Sunday night, I was back at Mommy's. When the phone rang, I dashed for it. "Girls can do anything!" I said.

"Karen?" It was Daddy's voice.

"Hi, Daddy."

"Hi, honey. I have a job for you. Elizabeth just thought of it. We need you to pull up dandelions in the backyard. Are you interested? I'll pay you ten cents for each dandelion you pull up *with* its roots. What do you think?"

"I'll take the job!" I cried.

After Daddy and I hung up the phone, I picked it right up again. I had to call Hannie with the news. But the doorbell rang. Then Nancy ran upstairs. "Karen, Karen! Great news!" she said. "I have a job!"

"You *do?* So do I!"

Nancy's job was to wash her parents' outdoor furniture.

"Now let's call Hannie," I said, but before we could, the phone rang.

It was Hannie! "I have a job!" she exclaimed. "My first one! Mommy and Daddy hired me!"

Cool. We all had work. The Doll Sisters were nearly ours.

# Dandelions

On Saturday, Seth drove me to Daddy's. It was not a big-house weekend, but I had a job to do. I was a working woman. I felt very important as I ran into the backyard with a bucket and a trowel.

"Let me show you something," said Daddy. He grabbed a dandelion and pulled at the leaves. "That is *not* how to get rid of a dandelion," he told me. "If you do not want the dandelion to come back, you have to pull up the roots, too. Like this. *But* you do not want to leave big holes all over the lawn. So use the trowel carefully."

"Okay," I replied. I looked at the dandelion Daddy was holding. "Do I get ten cents for that one?" I asked. "If *I* had pulled it up, I *might* have pulled up the roots, too."

Daddy grinned. "Okay. Ten cents." He handed me a pencil and a pad of paper. "Here. Use the paper to keep track of how many dandelions you pull up. Each time you get the roots, make a mark with the pencil."

Daddy left and I set to work. I tugged and dug and pulled until my arms ached. Then I tugged and dug and pulled some more.

Five, ten, fifteen . . . Dandelions were everywhere.

Twenty, twenty-five . . . I stopped to take a rest. I wiped my grubby hands on my jeans. I wiped my forehead. I sat up straight and stretched my back. And that was when I saw Morbidda Destiny.

The witch.

She was standing in her backyard. She

was looking in her garden. Most people grow flowers or vegetables in their gardens. The witch grows herbs. And then she uses them to make potions and cast spells. I am almost sure of this.

Quickly I turned around. I ran behind Daddy's flower garden. I knew the witch could not see me there. I just hoped I would find more dandelions. I did. A whole flock of them.

I tugged and dug and pulled. After a long, long time I thought I would not be able to pull up one more anything. So I took the pad and pencil and bucket and trowel into Daddy's house.

"Look!" I said. I held out the bucket. "I dug up thirty-one dandelions. With roots. They are all here."

"Wonderful, sweetheart!" said Daddy. "Great job!" And he paid me three dollars and ten cents. I felt gigundoly rich.

I stayed at Daddy's for lunch. In the afternoon, Hannie came over. "I earned two dollars," she said proudly. "I earned it by watching Sari for Mommy and Daddy while they were busy." (Sari is Hannie's baby sister.)

"Cool!" I said. "You are a baby-sitter."

"Well, sort of. Mommy and Daddy were at home. But still . . . I guess I am a baby entertainer. That's what I did. I entertained Sari. I even put her in her stroller and walked her up and down the driveway."

"I wonder what our next jobs will be," I said.

"*I* wonder how Nancy's job went."

"Let's call her," I said.

Nancy had hosed down *all* the Daweses' lawn furniture. The she had dried it with paper towels. It had been a big job. Her parents had paid her by the hour. Nancy had earned two dollars.

"Now how much money have we earned?" she asked.

Hannie added it up. "Seven-ten today," she replied. "Just thirty-one dollars to go."

# Karen's Red Face

At last, at last, at last. I was sitting in Miss Donovan's room at my gymnastics school. Today was the day we would find out who was going to be on the special invitational team.

I was sitting on the end of the balance beam. Class had not begun yet. I was supposed to be practicing. But I was too nervous to practice. How could I possibly think about balancing when — any minute now — Miss Donovan would be saying that soon I would be a star. I could see it now. The big sign in front of the Washington Mall would read: HELD OVER FOR ANOTHER WEEK! *Extra special gymnastics show. Starring the one and only* KAREN BREWER.

Or maybe I would use a stage name. Then the sign would read: *Starring the one and only* KATERINA VON DE BREWER! (That sounded exotic.)

As soon as everyone in the class had arrived, I raised my hand. "Miss Donovan, when are you going to tell us who is on the invitational team?"

"At the end of class, Karen."

"Oh, Miss Donovan, please, please, puh-*lease* can you tell us right now? I cannot wait a second longer. I don't think anyone else can, either."

"All right," said Miss Donovan. "I am happy to announce that three students in this class have been invited to join the team. They are . . ." (Miss Donovan paused. I closed my eyes.) ". . . Sophie."

"Yea!" cried Sophie.

"Gregg."

"Yes!" Gregg waved his fist in the air.

The last name was going to be mine. I knew it. I started to hop off the balance beam so I could be ready to jump up and cheer when Miss Donovan called my name. She called it while I was in mid-hop, and I didn't quite hear her, but so what?

I leaped in the air. "All right! I made it!" I shouted.

Natalie grabbed my hand. She pulled me onto the floor. "Miss Donovan didn't say your name!" she hissed. "She said Polly's name."

"She did?" I whispered. I looked around. Sophie, Gregg, and Polly were standing by Miss Donovan. They were grinning.

Everyone else was staring at me. I could feel my face turn red.

Oh, no. Oh, no. This was awful. I had made a fool of myself. But even worse, I

had *not* made the invitational team.

I would never get to perform in a mall.

That night at the little house I said, "Mommy, I do not think I can eat dinner. I am too, too sad."

"Just try," said Mommy.

I ate two pieces of corn on the cob and some fish and some salad and a peach and a dish of ice cream. But that was all.

Then I went into the bathroom. I looked at myself in the mirror. "Good-bye, Katerina von de Brewer," I said. I would not be needing my stage name.

I think Mommy overheard me. She said, "Karen? Let's have a little talk."

Mommy and I went to my bedroom. Seth came with us. "We know you are sad, honey," said Mommy. "But we are not disappointed in you. Neither is Daddy. You always try your best."

"That's right," said Seth. "Plus, you *can* do something about the team. You can practice. Maybe you will be asked to join next year."

That was it! I would practice, practice, practice, until I could turn the best cartwheel ever.

# Over and Over

I began practicing that very night. Right away, I changed my mind about something, though. I decided I did not need to practice until I could turn the best cartwheel ever. I just needed to practice until Miss Donovan said to me, "Karen, would you like to be on the team now? You are good enough to join." That was all I wanted. To be good enough to join the team.

When Mommy and Seth left my room, I stood by the doorway. I looked at the space between the door and my bed. Was it big enough to turn a cartwheel in? I thought so, but I was not sure. I had never tried it.

I stretched my hands in the air. Over I went. Bump! I landed with my back on the rug and my legs on the bed.

I guess there was not enough room.

I ran downstairs and stood at one end of the living room. It was empty. Mommy and Seth and Andrew were in the rec room. I decided there was plenty of space for cartwheels in the living room, so I turned one. When I landed on my feet, I was not even halfway across the room. So I turned another cartwheel and then another. Over and over and over I went. The cartwheels were not very good, but that was why I was practicing. Besides, I was getting faster. I had never turned three cartwheels in a row so quickly.

I decided to try it again. But I decided to try it through the hallway and into the rec room. I wanted to surprise my family.

I aimed myself for the entrance to the rec room. Over I went. And over and over — CRASH! I cartwheeled into Andrew.

"Ow!" he cried. He held his hand to his head. "Your foot hit my ear!"

"Karen, what *are* you doing?" asked Mommy.

"Practicing," I replied.

"How about practicing in the basement? I know we do not have tumbling mats, but at least the basement is carpeted now."

"Okay," I said. Then I added, "Sorry, Andrew."

After that, I practiced in the basement. The only thing I crashed into down there was the washing machine. (The dent I made was very small.) By the time I went to my next gymnastics class I could turn five cartwheels in a row without stopping.

I waited until class had ended. When Miss Donovan and I were the only people left in the room, I said, "Guess what. I have been practicing my cartwheels. Watch me!"

I chose the longest tumbling mat. I turned five cartwheels, from one end of the mat to the other. Over and over and over and over and over.

When I stood up I was wobbly and dizzy. But I could see that Miss Donovan was smiling. "Much better!" she said.

"Thank you," I replied politely. "May I be on the team now?"

I watched Miss Donovan's smile disappear. "Oh, Karen," she said. "I am sorry, but you are still not ready for the team. Your cartwheels are better. And they are certainly *faster*. But they are not good enough yet. You need to work some more. Anyway, we do not need more gymnasts on the team now. We have enough."

"Oh."

"We will choose new members in the fall."

"Oh."

"Karen, I really am sorry."

"Oh. I mean, I know you are. Thanks."

I walked into the hall where Seth was waiting for me. "How was your day?" he asked.

"Terrible," I answered.

# Cornelia, Cordelia, and Cecelia

Yea! The Three Musketeers had another job! This was a job for all of us to work on together. Elizabeth had phoned me at the little house one evening. "Our garage is a mess," she had said. "It's a pigsty." (I giggled.) "We cannot even park the cars in it anymore. Would you and Nancy and Hannie like to clean it out?"

"Oh, yes!" I exclaimed.

"It will be a big job."

"That's okay," I said. "We could do it on

49

Saturday. I mean, if Hannie and Nancy can come over then."

Both of my friends said they could go to the big house on Saturday. We decided to start work early, just in case the job lasted all day.

At nine o'clock we were in the garage. Daddy had rolled up the big doors for us. Then he had left us alone.

My friends and I looked around. Our garage is huge. It is not attached to our house. It is in our backyard, behind the trees and Daddy's gardens. The driveway in the front winds around to the side of the house and leads to the garage. All of the cars were parked in the driveway. None of them could fit in the garage.

"Look at all this *junk!*" cried Hannie. "I mean, sorry, Karen. It isn't junk exactly, but there is a lot of it. Whatever it is."

I laughed. "Most of it *is* junk, I think. Look at this." I held up a football. It was as flat as a pancake. There was a hole in the seam and the air had leaked out of it.

"Look at *this!*" cried Nancy. "What is it?"

Hannie and I rushed over to see. "Oh, gross!" said Hannie.

"That is Daddy's fish head," I said. "Once he caught this enormous fish. He was very proud of it, so he mounted its head on that board. Elizabeth says it is disgusting and that it cannot go in the house, but Daddy loves it. We better not throw that away."

"Can we throw away the football?" asked Nancy.

"Definitely," I said. "We can throw away lots of stuff."

We decided that everything we could throw away we would toss into the driveway. Soon a mountain of stuff was out there. We were working extra hard. But we were able to talk while we worked.

"I keep thinking about the Doll Sisters," said Nancy. "Then I do not mind our work. It is almost fun."

"I think about them, too," I said. "And I thought of a great new name for my doll. I have decided she should be Cornelia."

"Oh, pretty," said Hannie. "I think I will call my doll Cordelia."

"Then I will call mine Cecelia," said Nancy. "Aren't those beautiful names for triplets? Cornelia, Cordelia, and Cecelia. We —"

"SHHH!" I hissed. I was peering around a corner of the garage into Morbidda Destiny's backyard. "I see the witch!" I whispered.

"You do? Where?" said Hannie.

"Yeah, where?" said Nancy.

My friends did not see the witch, but I knew *I* had seen her. She had probably put a spell on herself to make her invisible to everyone except me. That is just the kind of sneaky witch thing she would do.

Nancy and Hannie and I went back to work. We took one break so I could show my friends my five fast cartwheels in a row. We did not finish cleaning that garage until lunchtime. The garage looked lovely. There was even room to park a car or two in it.

"Okay," I said, "now we get paid!"

# Working for the Witch

"Just a second," Nancy said. "I do not think we will get paid yet. The garage is lovely, but the driveway is not."

Nancy was right. That huge pile of junk was sitting in the driveway. There was so much I did not know what to do with it all.

"How are you coming along, girls?" Daddy and Elizabeth were walking across the backyard to the garage.

"Fine," Hannie said.

"We are finished," I said.

"We think," Nancy said.

I pointed to the stuff in the driveway. "We do not know what to do with that. The garbage people will not pick it up. Most of it is too big."

"Well," said Daddy, "I will drive it to the dump. Charlie and Sam can help me. You have done the hard part of the job. I guess you wouldn't want to get paid now, would you? You probably — "

"Oh, yes! We want to get paid!" I cried. *"Right* now."

Daddy gave each of us three dollars. *Nine* more dollars!

"Hannie! Get the money!" I exclaimed. "Let's count it again!"

Hannie flew across the street to her house. When she came back, she was carrying the sock. All of the money for the Doll Sisters was stuffed into it. Hannie was also carrying an old baby blanket. She spread the blanket on the ground. Then she emptied the sock onto it. Quarters and dimes and nickels and pennies and dollar bills fell out.

"Everyone add your three dollars," I ordered. We dropped the bills onto the little pile of money. I counted the dollars, and my friends counted the change. Then we added everything together.

"Hey, we have earned almost twenty dollars!" cried Nancy.

"Twenty-one to go," Hannie added. "Not bad."

"Yeah. We just need a few more jobs," I said. "Hannie? Do you think that your parents would like us to clean out *their* garage? If we cleaned out just two more really, really junky garages, we would have over thirty-seven dollars. We could probably get the Doll Sisters next weekend. I am sure Daddy would take us to the mall."

Hannie frowned. "I don't think my parents need us to clean the garage. Mommy did that a couple of months ago."

"Oh. I know! I could dig up some more dandelions."

"Psst! Karen!" Nancy interrupted me. "Here comes the witch!"

"Yipes!" I spun around.

There she was. Morbidda Destiny was walking slowly into our yard. She was coming from the direction of her herb garden.

"Hide!" I hissed, but we did not have enough time. I managed to hide our twenty dollars, though. I threw a corner of the blanket over the money. I did not want the witch to make it disappear.

"Hello!" called Morbidda Destiny.

"Save us," I whispered. But Hannie said, "Hello."

The witch smiled at my friends and me. "I read about your odd-job service," she said. "I saw a poster."

"Oh," I replied.

"I also saw you cleaning your father's garage, Karen." (I knew it!) "Guess what. My garage needs to be cleaned out, too. Would you girls like the job?"

I think my eyes nearly fell out of my head. Clean the *witch's* garage? Who knew what we might find? But Nancy and Hannie wanted the Doll Sisters very badly. So we said we would take the job.

# Broomsticks

"Can you come over right now?" Morbidda Destiny wanted to know.

My friends and I had not eaten lunch yet. I said we would come over in one hour.

We showed up right on time. It is important to be on time for any job, even if you are working for a witch.

Morbidda Destiny led us to her garage, which is attached to her house. She opened the door. I jumped back, but no bats flew out at me. All I could see was the witch's car and some other stuff. The garage was

59

not nearly as messy as Daddy and Elizabeth's.

"Just clean out the junk," said Morbidda Destiny. "And try to organize the other things." Then she went into her house.

"This does not look too bad," I said to Hannie and Nancy. "We will probably not earn nine dollars, but that is okay."

"Gosh, I wonder what a witch keeps in her garage," said Nancy.

We tiptoed around. We peeked in corners. We peered onto high shelves.

"Here is a cat carrier," I said. "It must be for her cat, Midnight. But why would she need a carrier? Doesn't Midnight fly around on her broom with her? Hmm."

"She could not take Midnight to the *vet* on a broomstick!" said Hannie. "She would have to put him in the carrier and drive her car."

Nancy was tossing out a pile of old rags. "Do you guys think Mrs. Porter is *really* a witch?" she asked us. (Mrs. Porter is what most people call Morbidda Destiny.)

"She looks like one," I said.

"She keeps brooms everywhere," said Hannie. "There are four just in the garage. I saw two more by the front door."

"She has hung baskets of herbs all over the place," added Nancy. "I suppose she is a witch."

I was sorting through Mrs. Porter's flowerpots. I put the broken ones next to the pile of rags. When that was finished, I began to take down the things that were jumbled together on a wooden shelf. There were some ratty old gardening gloves. There were two dented watering cans. There was a new bag of potting soil, a clock that did not work, some magazines, and a couple of thick black books. I began to open one of the books. Then I stopped. Wait a second! What if it was a book of spells? I should not even be touching it. I pulled my hands away. The book fell to the floor. THUD!

"What was that?" cried Hannie.

"Oh, a book!" Nancy ran for it. She started to pick it up.

"Don't!" I exclaimed. "That is witchy stuff. Leave it alone."

My friends and I worked and worked. The throwaway pile grew bigger. Soon we were finished. Except for that book. We left it on the floor. We were afraid to touch it.

"Well," I said. "Now what?"

"I guess one of us should get Mrs. Porter," said Nancy.

"Yeah, but which one of us?"

"Not me," said Hannie and Nancy.

"Don't look at me!" I exclaimed.

"Hello, girls!" called the witch. She whisked into the garage. Her black dress billowed around her. "Are you finished?"

"Yup," we said.

"Wonderful." Mobidda Destiny paid us six dollars.

"Fifteen to go," I said as Nancy and Hannie and I ran out of that garage.

We had almost reached the big house again when I saw someone hurrying down the sidewalk. Someone I knew well. And I got a terrific idea.

# Pretty Please

Guess who was walking down my street. Miss Donovan. I had forgotten that she lives in Daddy's neighborhood.

"You guys," I said to Hannie and Nancy, "I have to go somewhere. I just thought of something. Here. Take my money from the witch. Put it in the sock. And hide the sock well."

"Okay," my friends replied.

"Where are you going?" asked Hannie.

"Oh . . . just for a walk. If you see my

daddy, tell him I will be back soon. Tell him I did not go far away."

"All right," said Nancy. But her face looked like a question mark.

"We will be at my house," added Hannie.

I ran to the sidewalk. Then I walked toward Miss Donovan's house. On the way, I thought about cartwheels. I thought about gymnastics. I thought about the team. Maybe if I asked Miss Donovan really, really nicely she would let me join the team. Politeness must count for something.

When I reached Miss Donovan's house, I rang her bell.

"Karen!" she exclaimed when she opened the door.

"Hi, Miss Donovan," I said. "I was just in the neighborhood, so I thought I would drop by." (I have heard adults say that millions of times.)

"Well, I'm — I'm glad you did." (Miss

Donovan looked extra surprised.) "Would you like to come in?"

"Yes, thank you."

Miss Donovan and I sat in her living room. She gave me a cup of juice. I crossed my legs and tried to look grown-up. "Miss Donovan," I said, "I came over because . . . because . . ." Suddenly, I set my juice on the table. I stood up. I ran to one end of the living room. "I came because I want to show you my cartwheels again. I am still practicing. Watch." Over and over and over I went. Three VERY FAST cartwheels in a row. After the last one I landed on my bottom. But I got to my feet quickly. "There! How was that?"

"Pretty good," Miss Donovan answered.

*Pretty* good? Hmm. "Miss Donovan, I can do better. I don't *always* land on my bottom. I know I am good enough to join the team." I got ready to turn another cartwheel, but my teacher stopped me.

"Karen — " she began to say.

I interrupted her. "If you please, I would

very much like to join the team," I said. There. I did not think I could be more polite than that.

"Karen, you are not ready."

"But I am! I really think I am!" I exclaimed. "Also, I just *love* to perform. Audiences do not scare *me*. And the team gets to perform a lot."

"And compete," Miss Donovan reminded me. "You are not ready for competitions yet, Karen. Maybe someday, but not right now."

"I am ready to perform, though. I especially want to walk along the balance beam in Washington Mall."

"The team does not perform in malls," said Miss Donovan gently.

"It doesn't?" Oh. I felt a lump in my throat. It was growing bigger. Do not cry in front of Miss Donovan, I told myself. I drew in a deep breath. "Well, anyway, I did not *really* come over to show you cartwheels," I said. "I came to, um . . . I came to . . . to ask if you want me to do any odd jobs. My friends and I started an odd-job business. We need to earn money to buy some triplet dolls. Do you have any work for me?"

"Why, yes, I think I do," replied Miss Donovan.

15

# Weeding, Walking, Sweeping

Miss Donovan asked me to come over at nine o'clock the next morning. I arrived at eight-thirty in case she had extra work for me.

"Good morning!" I cried when Miss Donovan answered the door.

She was wearing her dressing gown and a pair of fuzzy slippers. She looked a teensy bit sleepy.

"I was not expecting you so early," she said. She was smiling, though.

"I am ready to work," I announced.

"And I can do anything. I am especially good at dandelion roots."

"Wonderful. Why don't you start on my dandelions, then? The yard is full of them. You can work on them before it gets too hot."

"Okay." I paused. Then I said, "I charge ten cents for each root. If I do not get the root, no charge."

"Fair enough," said Miss Donovan. She gave me a bucket, a trowel, and a pair of gardening gloves. "While you work, I will eat my breakfast."

Guess what. Miss Donovan ate her breakfast in the kitchen, and her kitchen windows face her backyard. So I pulled up four dandelion roots and then I turned four cartwheels. I stopped pretty often after that to turn more cartwheels. (I quit when Miss Donovan finished her breakfast and left the kitchen.)

When I could not see any more dandelions in the yard, I knocked on Miss Donovan's door. "I am finished with the roots,"

I told her, "and I did not leave big holes everywhere."

"Wonderful," said Miss Donovan. (But she did not say anything about my cartwheels.) "Now, how would you like to walk Station Wagon? Station Wagon is my poodle."

"Oh, I am very good at walking dogs."

I walked Station Wagon up the street to Daddy's house, and then back to Miss Donovan's. After that I swept the driveway and the patio. Then I watered the flower gardens. When I put the hose away, Miss Donovan said she had no more jobs for me. So she paid me for my work. I put the money in the pocket of my jeans.

Hmm. I have worked today, and Hannie and Nancy have not, I thought. I have earned more money for the Doll Sisters than either of them has. I wonder if that is fair.

# "I Am Hanging Up on You"

**W**hen I got home, I ran upstairs to my bedroom. I emptied the money out of my pocket. I laid it on the bedspread and counted it. Then I put it back into my pocket. I went across the street to Hannie's.

"Hi, Karen!" said my best friend.

"Hi. I have to talk to you."

"Okay." Hannie frowned.

"Where is the sock?" I asked. "We might be needing it."

Hannie and the sock and I went to Hannie's room. (Hannie had been hiding the sock inside a couch cushion in the living room. She said no one would ever find it there.)

"Is something wrong?" Hannie asked me.

I closed her door behind us. "Sort of," I replied. I showed her the money I had earned. "I worked at Miss Donovan's all morning," I said. "I worked really hard. And you know what? Altogether I have earned more than nine dollars, *not counting* the money from Miss Donovan. And you and Nancy have only earned about eight dollars each. So I think I should get to keep the money I made this morning. I mean, keep it for myself. I am ahead of you and Nancy."

"But you earned that money with our job business," said Hannie.

"So?"

"We agreed that we would save up *all* the money we earned so we could buy the Doll Sisters. We did not say anything about

keeping the money. Besides, Nancy and I thought up the business."

"Well, I named the business."

"Doesn't matter."

"Does too."

"Does not. Anyway, maybe Nancy and I will be getting some big jobs soon."

"Maybe you won't. Then *I* will end up paying for more than just one of the dolls. And that is not fair."

"It is not fair if you keep the money you earned."

"Let's call Nancy and ask her," I said. "I bet my *best* friend will say I should keep the money."

Nancy did say so!! I would not be needing the sock after all.

"I knew you would be on my side," I told her.

"It will just take us longer to get the Doll Sisters, that's all," Nancy continued. "Now we probably will not be able to buy them for eight weeks. Or maybe twelve weeks. That is three months, you know."

"You are being mean, Nancy!" I cried.

"So are you," she said.

"But I earned the money."

"Our deal was that you and Hannie and I would split anything we earned with our odd-job business."

"That is what Hannie said," I admitted. "Still, I earned the most money so far. More than you *or* Hannie."

"Mm-hmm."

"Well, I *did!*"

"I didn't say you didn't."

"Good-bye, Nancy," I said. "I am going to hang up on you now."

"No, you are not! I am hanging up on *you!*" And she did.

So I hung up on her, too, but she did not know it.

Then I shouted, "Good-*bye*, Hannie!" (She did not answer.) I ran out of Hannie's house. I ran back to Daddy's. I ran right through the house and into the backyard. And guess who I saw. Morbidda Destiny.

# The Witch's Secret

The witch was in her own backyard. She watched me run into mine. She watched me flump onto the ground under a tree.

I sat there and pouted.

"Hi, Karen!" called Morbidda Destiny.

I did not want to answer the witch, but I knew I had to. "Hi," I said.

"You and your friends did a wonderful job yesterday. My garage looks lovely. It is tidier than I have ever seen it."

"Thank you," I replied. (I could not smile.)

78

"Karen? Is something wrong?" asked the witch. "You look sad." She began to cross her yard. She was walking toward me!

I looked around. Where could I hide? Nowhere. The witch would see me wherever I went. So I just leaned against the tree.

"Karen?" asked Morbidda Destiny again. Now she was standing right next to me. She was looking at me. I could see a wart on her face. I could see hairs on her chin. Her long black dress was touching my knee. I edged away from her.

But since she was still waiting for an answer, I said, "I guess I am sad. See, my friends and I had a fight. We wanted to buy these dolls, so we were earning the money by doing odd jobs. I earned the most money. Then I wanted to keep some of it, so Hannie and Nancy and I had a fight. And the thing is, I cannot turn a cartwheel."

Morbidda Destiny looked confused. "You can't turn a cartwheel?"

"Not a very good one. So I was not asked

to join the special team at my gymnastics school. I wanted to perform at malls."

"I see." Morbidda did not look too sorry for me. Well, what can you expect from a witch? At least she was not smiling. "Karen, I do not understand just why you are so upset. You are very good at lots of things. You skipped into second grade at your school. You play softball on a team. You have been in a play. You have put on a carnival."

"I know. But I wanted to be good at gymnastics."

The witch frowned. Then she said, "I will tell you a secret. Wait right here until I come back."

The witch had a secret? Well, that was interesting. "Okay," I said.

Morbidda Destiny swished out of my yard. When she came back she was carrying something. Oh, no . . . It was the big, heavy book. It was the book of spells I had seen in her garage.

"Let me show you something," said Mor-

80

bidda. She sat down next to me. She started to open the book. I squinched my eyes shut.

But nothing happened.

"See this picture?" said the witch.

I opened my eyes. The book was a photo album! Morbidda Destiny was pointing to a picture of a girl on ice skates, whirling around in a rink. "That girl," said the witch, "is me." (It *was?*) "I used to compete as a skater. I won lots of medals." She flipped through the album and pointed to other pictures of herself as a skater. "But do you know what? I was never a good actress."

"Well, that's okay," I said.

Morbidda shook her head. "No. It wasn't. I *wanted* to be an actress, but I was not a good one. I loved the theater. I loved going to plays. But finally I had to accept the fact that the theater was fun for me. And that was all."

"But you were a good skater!" I cried.

"And you are a smart girl who can read

and write and play softball and run an odd-job business. And have fun in your gymnastics class," she added.

Oh, yeah. Morbidda was right. So I thanked her.

Then it was time to do something else.

# No More Fighting

Morbidda Destiny went back to her house — and I went back to Hannie's house. I did not *want* to go, but I knew I had to.

Hannie was in her yard with Linny. Linny was showing her how to catch a football. They were wearing football helmets.

"Hi, Hannie!" I called.

Hannie looked at me. Then she looked at Linny. "Okay, let her rip," she said. Linny threw the football. Hannie jumped up and caught it.

"Yea!" shouted Linny. "Good catch!"

"Hannie?" I said.

Hannie tossed the football to her brother. "I am not talking to you, Karen."

"You are now," I replied. "Anyway, I came over to say I'm sorry."

"Hey, did you two have a fight?" asked Linny.

"Yes," Hannie said.

"Sort of," I said.

"Oh, go ahead and make up," said Linny. Then he left.

"Hannie? I am really sorry," I began.

Hannie was still wearing the helmet. "I cannot hear you," she said.

"You could hear me before. Just listen."

"Okay, okay." Hannie and I sat down on the grass.

"I know I was being mean," I said. "But I think I was mad about something else. I think I was mad because I did not make the gymnastics team. Except I yelled at you and Nancy. That was not fair. Anyway, here is the money I earned at Miss Dono-

van's." I pulled it out of my pocket. "Let's go add it to the sock."

Hannie smiled at me. "All right."

We stuffed my money into the sock. Then I telephoned Nancy. I told her I was sorry, too. I said I wanted to buy the Doll Sisters *very soon*.

Our fight was over.

Two days later, Hannie entertained Sari again. The next day, Nancy washed her mother's car. The day after that, I baby-sat (entertained) Andrew, Nancy became a plant-sitter, and Hannie took her neighbor's dog for a walk. Jobs were turning up everywhere. Finally, Hannie called me at the little house one night.

"Karen!" she exclaimed. "You will not believe this! I just counted the money in the sock. We have forty-four dollars and ninety cents!"

"Oh, my gosh! That is excellent! We can buy the Doll Sisters!"

"We can even pay the tax on them," added Hannie.

I ran next door to Nancy's house. I told her the good news.

"Yea! When do you think we can go back to the mall?"

"I will call Daddy and find out."

"Goody."

That night I phoned Daddy at the big house. He said he would drive my friends and me to Washington Mall on Saturday. He said it would be a special trip for the Three Musketeers. No one else would go with us. (Especially no brothers, big or little.) We decided to leave at ten o'clock in the morning.

On Friday, Hannie and Nancy and I talked about our dolls' names.

"What do you guys *really* think about Cornelia, Cordelia, and Cecelia?" I asked.

Nancy scrunched up her nose. Hannie frowned.

We renamed the Doll Sisters. We decided on Katie, Becky, and Laura.

**19**

# Terry, Kerry, and Merry

"Daddy, are we almost there yet?" I asked.

Daddy glanced at me in the rearview mirror. "I can still see your mother's house," he replied. "We have not left your street."

"Oh, yeah," I said.

Saturday morning had finally arrived. It was Doll Sisters' Day! Daddy was driving Nancy and Hannie and me to Washington Mall. He was in the front seat. My friends and I were buckled into the backseat. Hannie was sitting in the middle, holding our sock.

"Are you *sure* we have enough money?" Nancy asked Hannie. "Are you positive?"

"I counted it twice last night," Hannie replied. "Don't worry."

The Three Musketeers did not worry. But we were not very patient. The closer we got to the Doll Sisters, the faster we wanted to be *with* them.

"Daddy, can you drive faster?" I said.

"Please settle down, Karen," he answered.

I think we drove for about six months before we reached the mall. When Daddy had parked the car, we ran inside. Even Daddy ran.

This time we did not poke through the stores. We did not ask for a treat to eat. We did not look around for gymnasts. We walked straight to Toy Palace. And I marched right up to the salesman.

"Where are the dolls, please?" I asked. "We are in a hurry."

"Aisle seven," said the salesman.

"Thank you."

Nancy began to frown. "What if the Doll Sisters are all gone?" she asked. "Or what if only *two* are left? That would be horrible!"

When my friends and I found aisle seven we stood at one end. We looked up one side and down the other.

"Do you remember seeing so many dolls the last time?" I asked.

"No," said Nancy.

"No," said Hannie.

I felt as worried as Nancy looked. But Daddy said, "There is just one thing to do. We will walk down the aisle very slowly and look at every doll. If we do not see the Doll Sisters, we will ask for help."

"Okay," said Hannie and Nancy and I.

We walked by dolls that talked and dolls that smiled and dolls that burped. We walked by dolls with fair skin and dolls with dark skin, dolls with brown eyes and green eyes and blue eyes. We walked by baby dolls and teenaged dolls and doll families.

We had almost reached the end of the aisle.

"There they are!" shrieked Nancy just then. "There they are!"

"Where?" asked Daddy.

"There!"

I could see about ten Doll Sisters lined up in their boxes.

"There?" said Daddy. "You mean those dolls? But they are called Terry Dolls, not the Doll Sisters."

"We know," I said. "We are going to buy three Terry Dolls and *make* them the Doll Sisters. They will be triplets."

Hannie and Nancy and I each chose one Terry Doll. We were careful to choose dolls with the same hair color and the same outfits. They looked exactly alike. Then we paid for them. Hannie dumped the sock onto the counter by the cash register. She and Nancy and I counted out the money.

The next thing we knew, the Doll Sisters were ours.

We named them Terry, Kerry, and Merry.

**20**

# The Giggles

One day when I went to my gymnastics class, I found a surprise. Three new kids were sitting on the balance beam. They were watching Jannie and Natalie and Gemma, who were tumbling on the mats.

I walked right over to the new kids. "Who are you?" I asked.

"I'm Douglas," said one.

"I'm Wesley," said one.

"I'm Clara," said one.

"Hi, I'm Karen. Are you going to be in my class now?"

"Yup," they answered.

"Well, are you any good at cartwheels?"

"No," said Douglas.

"Yes," said Wesley.

"Sort of," said Clara.

Miss Donovan clapped her hands then. "Boys and girls, today three students have joined our class." She introduced them to the rest of us. (I bet she was glad she could say "*boys* and girls" now and mean it.) "Also," my teacher went on, "I have a surprise for you. In a few minutes we are going to go to another room. We will be able to watch the invitational team for a little while. I thought you would like to see how Polly and Gregg and Sophie are doing. They will be going to their first meet soon."

I wished I could go with them. I really did. I even started to ask Miss Donovan — just one more time — if she would *please* let me be on the team. But before I could, Miss Donovan was leading us out of our room and into the hall. We walked next door and sat in a row on a blue tumbling

95

mat. In front of us stood Gregg, Polly, Sophie, and about fifteen other kids. Some of those kids were *big* (maybe twelve years old). And they all got to wear very cool red, white, and blue team uniforms.

Well, guess what. Right away I realized I could not be on that team. Not then, anyway. Those kids were extra good gymnasts. The older ones could fly over the horse. The boys flipped around on the rings. One girl could do all sorts of turns and flips on the uneven bars. And Sophie was learning a very fancy way to dismount when she was finished on the balance beam. Even if I learned how to turn a perfect cartwheel, I would not be ready for the invitational team. Miss Donovan had been right.

After awhile we went back to our own classroom. Natalie and I decided to make up a floor routine. We put forward rolls and backward rolls and leaps into it. At the end of the routine, I turned my five fast cartwheels in a row while Natalie hummed

"I'm Flying" from *Peter Pan*. We kept giggling. Gymnastics was fun, even if I was not very good.

Seth picked me up when class was over. Guess what. He was carrying Terry. (Terry is *my* Doll Sister.) "I have a surprise for you," he said. "It is waiting in the car."

"Oh, boy!" I shrieked. I grabbed Seth's hand and pulled him to the parking lot. Waiting in the car were Hannie and Nancy. Hannie was holding Kerry, and Nancy was holding Merry.

Seth unlocked the car. He slid into the driver's seat. I slid into the backseat with my friends. I held up Terry. "Hi, Merry! Hi, Kerry!" I made her say. Then Nancy and Hannie and the Doll Sisters and I headed for home.

## About the Author

ANN M. MARTIN lives in New York City and loves animals, especially cats. She has two cats of her own, Mouse and Rosie.

Other books by Ann M. Martin that you might enjoy are *Stage Fright*; *Me and Katie (the Pest)*; and the books in *The Baby-sitters Club* series.

Ann likes ice cream and *I Love Lucy*. And she has her own little sister, whose name is Jane.

## Little Sister

Don't miss #30

### KAREN'S KITTENS

I hurried into the kitchen. I filled a bowl with water and a plate with some of Boo-Boo's cat food. I did not bother asking Boo-Boo first. Since he was such a mean old cat, he probably would not want to share.

I raced back to the toolshed. On the way, I tripped over a rock and spilled everything. Boo. I had to pick up all the food, then go back and fill the bowl with water again.

I hoped the cat would not have her kittens before I got back to the shed.

She didn't. I was starting to feel really lucky. It had started out a boring Saturday. But it was not boring anymore. And I had wanted a cat or a kitten. Now I was going to have some!

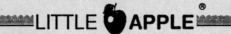

# LITTLE APPLE®

# BABY·SITTERS

## Little Sister™

### by Ann M. Martin, author of *The Baby-sitters Club* ®

| | | | |
|---|---|---|---|
| ☐ | MQ44300-3 | #1 | Karen's Witch | $2.75 |
| ☐ | MQ44259-7 | #2 | Karen's Roller Skates | $2.75 |
| ☐ | MQ44299-6 | #3 | Karen's Worst Day | $2.75 |
| ☐ | MQ44264-3 | #4 | Karen's Kittycat Club | $2.75 |
| ☐ | MQ44258-9 | #5 | Karen's School Picture | $2.75 |
| ☐ | MQ44298-8 | #6 | Karen's Little Sister | $2.75 |
| ☐ | MQ44257-0 | #7 | Karen's Birthday | $2.75 |
| ☐ | MQ42670-2 | #8 | Karen's Haircut | $2.75 |
| ☐ | MQ43652-X | #9 | Karen's Sleepover | $2.75 |
| ☐ | MQ43651-1 | #10 | Karen's Grandmothers | $2.75 |
| ☐ | MQ43650-3 | #11 | Karen's Prize | $2.75 |
| ☐ | MQ43649-X | #12 | Karen's Ghost | $2.75 |
| ☐ | MQ43648-1 | #13 | Karen's Surprise | $2.75 |
| ☐ | MQ43646-5 | #14 | Karen's New Year | $2.75 |
| ☐ | MQ43645-7 | #15 | Karen's in Love | $2.75 |
| ☐ | MQ43644-9 | #16 | Karen's Goldfish | $2.75 |
| ☐ | MQ43643-0 | #17 | Karen's Brothers | $2.75 |
| ☐ | MQ43642-2 | #18 | Karen's Home-Run | $2.75 |
| ☐ | MQ43641-4 | #19 | Karen's Good-Bye | $2.75 |
| ☐ | MQ44823-4 | #20 | Karen's Carnival | $2.75 |
| ☐ | MQ44824-2 | #21 | Karen's New Teacher | $2.75 |
| ☐ | MQ44833-1 | #22 | Karen's Little Witch | $2.75 |
| ☐ | MQ44832-3 | #23 | Karen's Doll | $2.75 |
| ☐ | MQ44859-5 | #24 | Karen's School Trip | $2.75 |
| ☐ | MQ44831-5 | #25 | Karen's Pen Pal | $2.75 |
| ☐ | MQ44830-7 | #26 | Karen's Ducklings | $2.75 |
| ☐ | MQ44829-3 | #27 | Karen's Big Joke | $2.75 |
| ☐ | MQ44828-5 | #28 | Karen's Tea Party | $2.75 |
| ☐ | MQ44825-0 | #29 | Karen's Cartwheel | $2.75 |
| ☐ | MQ43647-3 | | Karen's Wish   Super Special #1 | $2.95 |
| ☐ | MQ44834-X | | Karen's Plane Trip   Super Special #2 | $2.95 |
| ☐ | MQ44827-7 | | Karen's Mystery  Super Special #3 | $2.95 |

**Available wherever you buy books, or use this order form.**

**Scholastic Inc., P.O. Box 7502, 2931 E. McCarty Street, Jefferson City, MO 65102**

Please send me the books I have checked above. I am enclosing $_____
(please add $2.00 to cover shipping and handling). Send check or money order - no cash
or C.O.Ds please.

Name_____

Address_____

City_____State/Zip_____

Please allow four to six weeks for delivery. Offer good in U.S.A. only. Sorry, mail orders are not
available to residents to Canada. Prices subject to change.

BLS991

# Kristy is Karen's older stepsister, and she and her friends are...

## by Ann M. Martin, author of *Baby-sitters Little Sister*™

| | | |
|---|---|---|
| ❑ NM43388-1 # 1 | Kristy's Great Idea | $3.25 |
| ❑ NM43513-2 # 2 | Claudia and the Phantom Phone Calls | $3.25 |
| ❑ NM43512-4 # 4 | Mary Anne Saves the Day | $3.25 |
| ❑ NM43720-8 # 5 | Dawn and the Impossible Three | $3.25 |
| ❑ NM43899-9 # 6 | Kristy's Big Day | $3.25 |
| ❑ NM43509-4 # 8 | Boy-Crazy Stacey | $3.25 |
| ❑ NM43508-6 # 9 | The Ghost at Dawn's House | $3.25 |
| ❑ NM43387-3 #10 | Logan Likes Mary Anne! | $3.25 |
| ❑ NM43569-8 #46 | Mary Anne Misses Logan | $3.25 |
| ❑ NM44971-0 #47 | Mallory on Strike | $3.25 |
| ❑ NM43571-X #48 | Jessi's Wish | $3.25 |
| ❑ NM44970-2 #49 | Claudia and the Genius of Elm Street | $3.25 |
| ❑ NM44969-9 #50 | Dawn's Big Date | $3.25 |
| ❑ NM44968-0 #51 | Stacey's Ex-Best Friend | $3.25 |
| ❑ NM44966-4 #52 | Mary Anne + 2 Many Babies | $3.25 |
| ❑ NM44967-2 #53 | Kristy for President | $3.25 |
| ❑ NM44240-6 | Baby-sitters on Board! Super Special #1 | $3.50 |
| ❑ NM44239-2 | Baby-sitters' Summer Vacation Super Special #2 | $3.50 |
| ❑ NM43973-1 | Baby-sitters' Winter Vacation Super Special #3 | $3.50 |
| ❑ NM42493-9 | Baby-sitters' Island Adventure Super Special #4 | $3.50 |
| ❑ NM43575-2 | California Girls! Super Special #5 | $3.50 |
| ❑ NM43576-0 | New York, New York! Super Special #6 | $3.50 |
| ❑ NM44963-X | Snowbound Super Special #7 | $3.50 |